THE REAL GHOSTBUSTERS

The Revenge of Murray the Mantis

Maureen Spurgeon

CARNIVAL

The Real Ghostbusters sat around forlornly looking at the fridge. All they saw was some thing better left unmentioned. Egon stood sniffing at one particularly revolting tub of slime.

"Mmmm. . . a rare example of *conferva pulverulens aquatica.* Splendid!"

"Yeah, great Egon," snarled Ray, "but what are we going to eat for our Thanksgiving dinner, huh? Somehow Fungus Fritters don't appeal. How come we never have any food in this place?"

Slimer, the resident green ghoul, hearing the word 'food', hurtled round the fire station opening drawers and turning over boxes, his mouth open, expectantly.

"I guess there's your answer," sighed Winston. "I bought this turkey yesterday — mouth-wateringly wonderful. Looks like that greaseball ate it."

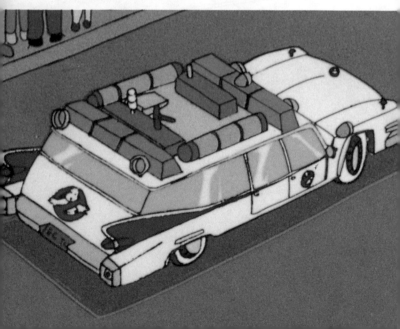

"All I hope," said Peter Venkman solemnly, "is that he hasn't trailed green gunk over the Ectomobile. Not after I spent most of yesterday on my knees polishing it to perfection."

The Ghostbusters' Ectomobile had never looked so good. The windows, the headlamps, the paintwork— even the chrome and hub caps were shining bright.

"Wait till the kids see us in the Thanksgiving Day Parade, tomorrow!" Ray Stantz declared, "We'll be the coolest, neatest outfit there."

"As long as Slimer doesn't decide to come along!" added Winston Zeddmore.

"Oh, I don't know. . . " Egon Spengler seemed thoughtful. "Slimer can be quite useful at times. . . "

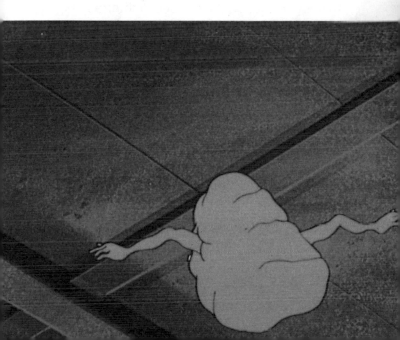

All over the city similar preparations were going on. Clothes were pressed, cakes baked – and in one cold, draughty warehouse, a huge balloon was being filled with air from an electric pump. Every so often, a smartly-dressed young women cast nervous glances at the long cobwebs that swayed creepily from rusting beams. She shuddered as out of the dark filthy shadows, green rats' eyes glittered.

"I'll be glad when you finish this job for my T.V. company!" she told one of the workmen. "This place gives me the shivers!"

"You and me both!" The man trembled. "Who can forget this warehouse was built over an old graveyard?"

An uneasy silence descended, lightened only by the chugging of the pump engine and the wooden floorboards creaking underneath.

Then, as the engine chugged on, a crack in the floor began to widen, glowing with a deep red light. Wisps of pinkish gas began to float up from below and into the air pump filling the balloon. . . Next day, the weather was perfect for a Thanksgiving Parade, lots of people were out on the streets enjoying the fun – including green-ghostie Slimer, hitching a ride in the Ghostbusters' Ectomobile, after all!

"I'm not sitting all squashed up in here the whole time!" Janine announced, eyes glaring behind her horn-rimmed glasses. "Someone has to get out!"

"How about riding on the roof?" Peter suggested, "I wouldn't mind trying it!"

"Me, neither!" cried Ray, already scrambling up. "Come on, Peter, enjoy the view!"

"Ray, why are you always such a big kid?" Peter asked. But he smiled as he said it, waving to the crowds from his roof-top seat.

The parade was suddenly thrown into darkness by an enormous shadow. Peter and Ray looked up together, startled.

"What the blazes is that thing?" wondered Peter, shielding his eyes. "Whoever heard of a hundred foot long, lime green insect wearing a pork-pie hat and speckled bow-tie?"

Ray gave a shriek of excitement.

"Hey, Egon, take a look! It's our favourite T.V. cartoon character, Murray the Mantis!"

"The Murray the Mantis Show is the best thing on Saturday morning television!" Ray explained to an astonished Peter. "Murray lives in this garden, see – he's a sort of sheriff that keeps the peace and chases away all the bad guys!"

"Yeah! Like the Evil Hypno-Snake and the Giant Slug Brothers!" Egon shouted up. "He's the best friend of the gardener's little girl, Posy!"

"You mean you actually watch that stuff, Egon?" Peter could hardly believe his ears. "Someone with a brilliant scientific mind, like yours?"

"Remember, Venkman," replied Egon, a trifle huffily, "the brain of a good scientist must be enriched by creative imagination!"

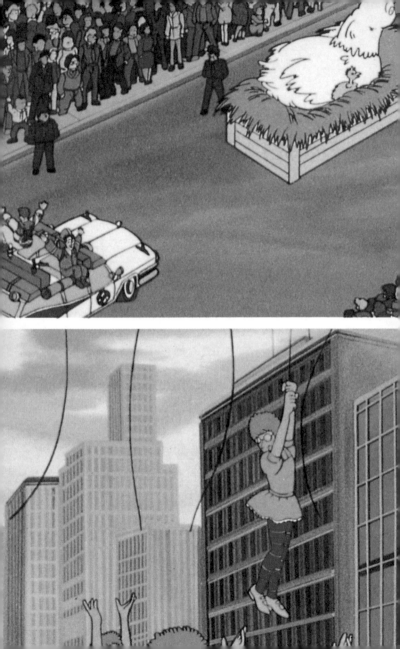

Ray gazed up at Murray the Mantis with a big, stupid grin on his face. Then, just for one moment, it crossed his mind that he might have seen a soft, greeny glow appearing in one of the seams of the balloon – but no, he decided, he must have been mistaken.

It was a fine morning, everyone was smiling and having a wonderful time at the Thanksgiving Day Parade. . . Some of the floats were outrageous, was that a chicken or what?

A traffic policeman was signalling for the Ectomobile to slow down, Winston leaned out of the driver's window.

"Hi there, Officer Frump! What's the hold-up?"

"They're having some problem with that Murray the Mantis right behind you! Too much gas inside, I reckon!"

Peter and Ray glanced questioningly at each other, then over their shoulders.

"Can you see how fast that thing's rising?" bellowed Peter. "It's taking off, all by itself!"

"And the people in the ground crew!" bawled Officer Frump. "They're being pulled into the air with it!"

The young woman from the television company pushed her way through the crowds, dashing up to Officer Frump and snatching his megaphone, her voice booming out above all the noise and commotion.

"Let it go! Let go of Murray the Mantis!"

Hearing her instructions, the crew-men dropped their ropes, falling back to the ground as Murray the Mantis soared up high above the New York skyline.

"That thing," growled Officer Frump, fast regaining his stern air of authority, "is now a menace to low-flying aircraft!"

"Oh no! You're right – it is!" the T.V. woman agreed with a moan. She turned anxiously towards the Ghostbusters.

"You've got those Proton things, haven't you?

Couldn't you shoot it down, somehow?"

"Consider it done, lady!" Peter was always quick at turning on the charm. "Toasted green stuff, coming right up!"

He knelt down and fired his Proton Gun towards the sky, an ion beam streaking right into the balloon, dead on target.

"But," gulped Winston, "it – it's not exploding!"

"No, it's getting bigger, instead!" shouted Spengler, hands over his ears. "Here comes the big bang!"

As he spoke, the balloon burst open – revealing a giant, green Murray the Mantis, his great mouth wide open in a roar which seemed to threaten the whole city.

The panic-stricken crowds seemed like tiny ants fleeing from the great, green bulk of Murray the Mantis, which was coming closer every second.

"Up here, lady!" shouted Ray Stantz, half lifting, half tugging the T.V. woman on to the roof of the Ectomobile. "Come on, Peter! Get back with us!"

Between them, they both managed to make a grab at Venkman's wrists, hauling him to safety.

He was still clinging precariously to the roof as the menacing shadow of Murray the Mantis swept overhead. Winston vaulted back into the driving seat of the Ectomobile and they speeded away, sirens wailing.

"Did I cause that?" panted Peter, scrambling up beside Ray and his female passenger.

"No." Ray shook his head in confusion. "Our

equipment just doesn't work that way."

"Then," said the T.V. woman after a pause, "it must have been us." She took a deep breath. "We filled that balloon in an old warehouse which was built right over a graveyard!"

"That's it!" cried Ray. "A release of dormant energy!"

"You'll soon get used to him," Peter smiled. "By the way, I'm Doctor Peter Venkman!"

"And I'm Anne Lawson."

"I'm getting a Psycho Kinetic Energy reading from the PKE meter!" Egon broke in. "We're heading for big trouble!"

Spengler was always right. For there, right in the path of the Ghostbuster's Ectomobile, Murray the Mantis hovered high above a tall line of trees.

"Get into reverse gear, Winston!" ordered Venkman. This thing needs working on!"

Back at HQ, Egon began tapping keys on his computer.

"We cross index the size of the balloon with that of the standard praying mantis. . . And that gives us. . . "

"Absolutely nothing!" Venkman burst out impatiently. "What about getting Slimer on the job? He can talk spooks' language, being one himself!"

Slimer floated down in front of Peter, shaking his head fearfully.

"Aw, come on, my little green pal!" coaxed Peter. "You can have that little refrigerator you wanted – remember? Ice cream every day, cool fizzy drinks. . ."

Slimer nodded eagerly, kissing Venkman on the nose, leaving a great dollop of green, sticky stuff.

"Ye-e-e-uk--!" he screeched out. "Slimer!"

But Slimer was already sliding down to the basement with Egon, sirens wailing in the street and getting nearer.

There was a terrified scream from Janine.

"The police are right outside! They must think it's all your fault! Oh, what shall I do?"

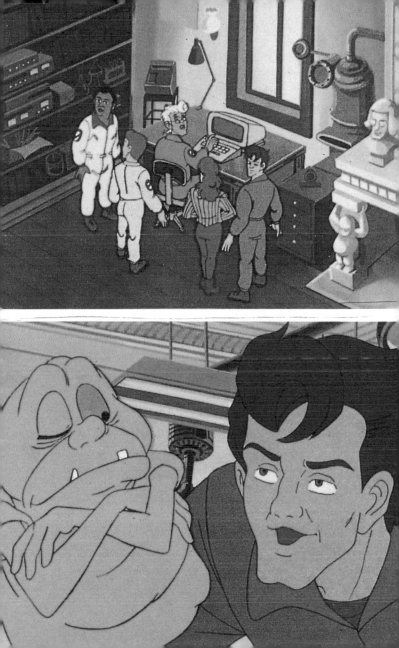

Before anyone could make any sensible suggestions, the door was kicked open, and Egon Spengler found himself in the grip of two burly Officers of the Law.

"Outside, along with the rest of your friends! Officer Frump just can't wait to meet you all again!"

There was a sudden, loud rumble, making the earth shudder beneath their feet.

"Our containment unit in the basement!" yelled Venkman in alarm. "It's about to blow up!"

He grabbed Anne Lawson's hand, pulling her to safety behind the police car only seconds before the roof of the old fire station was blown off in a spray of ghostly ectoplasm which rose up into the sky, forming an enormous, glowing cloud. It seemed disturbingly familiar.

"Would you look at that!" gasped Egon Spengler. "Do you see what I see, Ray?"

"Seems like someone we've met before!" shouted Stantz, beginning to smile. "That roly-poly face! The sailor suit! That cute, chubby grin. . ."

"Not the Stay-Puft Marshmallow Man!" groaned Officer Frump, following their gaze. "Are you Ghostbuster guys crazy?"

"That's a matter of opinion," shrugged Peter Venkman, still looking up at the sky. "I knew we couldn't handle it ourselves, so I released him."

"I think," said Ray slowly, "that this is where Slimer can help us." He turned to the policeman. "Any chance of a lift in a helicopter, Officer?"

Stay-Puft was enjoying a gentle stroll through the park by the time the Ghostbusters caught up with him, not even looking up at the helicopter overhead.

Spengler was speaking into his radio transmitter as the Stay-Puft Marshmallow Man came into sight.

"Come in, Great Green One!" He looked out to see Slimer climbing up under Stay-Puft's sailor hat, complete with head-phones.

"Stay with him, Slimer!" Egon continued over the radio. Slimer nodded in reply. "And keep him heading north!"

Murray the Mantis was still looming over the trees, rather like a boat sailing on a sea of green. He had already snapped up a hot-dog stand in his jaws, tossing it away in disgust. Now he was looking for another snack. Maybe, he thought, a little car which he happened to see driving along on its own . . .

"D'you think we should have dodged all those police blockades, Earl?"

"Sure, why not?" the driver demanded. "It's the perfect chance to enjoy a nice, peaceful day out!"

He spoke too soon. Next minute, a sinister-looking shadow threw itself over the car and a gigantic, monster-size mouth gaped wide open.

The driver gave a shriek and grabbed his girlfriend, just in time. "Come on!" he yelled. "Let's get out of here!"

Murray the Mantis could hardly wait to take the first delicious bite. But – ugh! He spat out the entire mouthful! Small cars, he thought, tasted even worse than hot-dog stands!

Perhaps he would have more luck with that helicopter, flying right overhead . . .

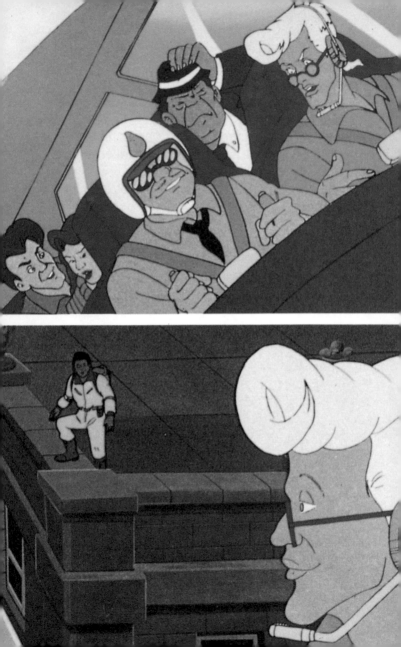

With one gigantic leap, Murray the Mantis had sprung high into the air, spreading out his huge wings and was sweeping in straight towards the police helicopter.

"Get moving, pal!" Venkman urged the pilot. "Time to go into a climb!"

In a race against time, the helicopter rose higher and higher. Murray the Mantis meanwhile was crashing into yet another cluster of trees, scattering leaves and branches everywhere.

From the ground, Winston and Ray got ready with their Proton Packs and the Ghostbusters' own helicopter, ECTO-TWO.

"Hey, Winston!" yelled Ray, jerking his head up. "Here comes the police chopper landing right beside our Ectomobile!"

"Great!" pronounced Zeddmore. "Now we can go into action!"

Murray the Mantis was in an ugly mood by now, storming around looking for something to eat, uprooting trees — and certainly paying no attention to either of the helicopters hovering around at a safe distance.

Thanks to Ray Stantz and ECTO-TWO, Winston was positioned on top of a tall building at the edge of the park, armed with his Proton Pack. He waved frantically across to Egon Spengler, who had been lowered on to another building from the police helicopter.

"Come in Ray!" ordered Spengler, speaking into his walkie-talkie radio.

"Go ahead, Egon," came the voice of Ray Stantz over the radio from the cockpit of ECTO–TWO.

"We're all ready," Egon told him. "Good luck to you and to Peter!"

Venkman was too busy waving goodbye to Anne Lawson from the open door of the helicopter to hear this last remark. So it was quite a shock when the rotor blades began whirling and the helicopter shot up in the air.

"He--e-e-e-y???!" he screamed, being thrown back in his seat. "How about taking some pilot lessons?"

"Take it easy!" Ray protested. "I'm pretty good for a guy who's never done this sort of thing before!"

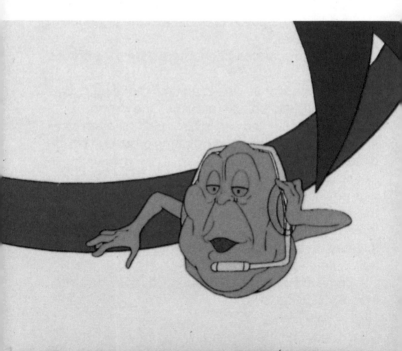

"Look!" he yelled, staring down through the cockpit windscreen. "There's our friend, Murray the Mantis! And the Stay-Puft Man's right on his tail!"

"Terrific!" Venkman was not too impressed. "Now, what?"

"We shoot him if he tries to fly off somewhere!"

Slimer was also there, giving hurriedly whispered instructions right into the Stay-Puft Man's ear as he lumbered on, through a patch of woodland and into a meadow.

Murray the Mantis had reached the meadow, too, he raised his enormously heavy front legs, then charged across the grass running straight into Stay-Puft his enormous claws raised for the kill.

"Ugh!" Venkman cried out with a shudder. "Did you see the way that thing clawed Stay-Puft's marshmallow arms with those great legs of his! Hey, Murray the Mantis! Fight fair!"

But Stay-Puft was not a marshmallow man to be beaten easily. With slow deliberation, he swung back his left arm, landing a powerful punch which lifted Murray the Mantis off his feet and sent him sprawling on his back, legs waving wildly in the air. There was a resounding cheer from Peter Venkman.

"Great stuff, Marshmallow Man! Show him he can't have things all his own way!"

"Get ready to fire, Winston," urged Ray. "This is our chance to hit him!"

Ion beams from Zeddmore's Proton Gun streaked out, hitting Murray the Mantis and forcing him to the ground once more, giving one last wailing shriek as the helicopter whirled up out of his reach.

Egon Spengler was watching the whole thing from his position on top of the building. Through his binoculars, he could see Stay-Puft lumbering towards Murray the Mantis yet again, with Murray darting in and out of his marshmallow legs, trying to bite him.

Just a little further along, the Ghostbusters' Ectomobile came into view, with someone waving up to him.

"Right," said Spengler, speaking into his radio for the last time. "Bring him in. We're ready."

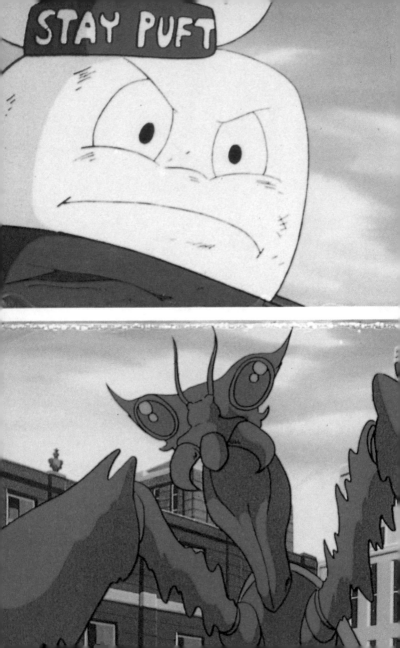

The Stay-Puft Man was still in the fight, but Murray the Mantis was working himself up into a furious temper, taking bites out of him wherever he could, so that Stay-Puft had to keep backing away. Slimer was quick to point out to him that Murray's great jaws were fast getting gummed up with marshmallow – but, all the same, Stay-Puft Man was mightily relieved when the mantis had to retreat, unable to bite any longer.

Peter Venkman siezed this chance to fire once again from the doorway of ECTO-TWO, when a huge splatter of white marshmallow spurted out from the mouth of Murray the Mantis.

"Peter, I can't see!" Ray cried out from the cockpit. "There's a great blob of white goo covering the windscreen!"

"Marshmallow . . ." Peter groaned. "Don't you have any wipers on this thing?"

"No!" Ray roared, frantically working the controls. "You'll have to clean it off from the outside!"

Peter Venkman said nothing. Just raised his Proton Gun and fired.

The windscreen shattered into a milion pieces which were at once sucked away into the air outside like thousands of starry snowflakes. Stantz and Venkman both opened their eyes again at the same moment.

"Thanks, Peter," Ray said dolefully. "There's nothing like doing the right thing at the right time . . ."

"Hold on!" he yelled again, yanking on the joystick. "We're coming up to Egon!"

"Get down, Spengler!" yelled Venkman. The helicopter was swooping too low for comfort.

Throwing himself flat on the roof of the building, Egon caught sight of Murray the Mantis backing away into a courtyard below. He fumbled for his walkie-talkie.

"Winston . . ." he whispered,

"Okay," Winston answered him over his radio. "Let's fry this grasshopper!"

Within seconds, Egon and Winston were ready to fire. Murray the Mantis continued to edge his way into the courtyard. Meanwhile Stay-Puft was advancing towards Murray the Mantis with Ray Stantz and Peter Venkman tumbling out of the

helicopter, clutching their Proton Guns behind him.

"Now!" came Egon Spengler's voice over the walkie-talkie.

The Ghostbusters opened fire, hitting Murray the Mantis from all sides, Stay-Puft helping by reaching out for the monster and holding him still.

"Keep it going!" bellowed Venkman, shooting fast.

"But don't hit Stay-Puft!" shouted Ray Stantz in childlike concern. "Look, Murray the Mantis is beginning to flicker! He's getting weaker!"

"He's about to explode," corrected Spengler, watching the bright green glow merging into red. "Watch out!"

There was a blinding, white flash – and Murray the Mantis had gone.

It had all been so tiring for Stay-Puft that he could only stagger around wearily. Even green-ghostie Slimer dropped down with a tired moan and fell asleep right where he landed.

"Is it all over?" queried Ray, crawling out from behind the Ectomobile, the paint on one side blackened and blistered.

"No," replied Venkman. "I think I'm still alive!"

"Peter!" came the cry from Anne Lawson. "Peter, you were wonderful!"

It was enough to turn any Ghostbuster's head.

"You were pretty wonderful, yourself!"

"Never mind the congratulations!" Officer Frump interrupted grumpily. "What about this Thanksgiving Day Parade?"

"And this time," said Anne Lawson, smiling up at Venkman, "I'm riding on the roof!"

Slimer was there too, enjoying his place of honour – even though the cheering crowds lining the streets for the parade couldn't see him!

"Boy, this is great!" beamed Venkman. "Too bad about your Murray the Mantis balloon, Anne!"

"That's all right," Anne beamed. "After all, you did find a wonderful replacement!"

And the Stay-Puft Marshmallow Man, floating high above the admiring crowds, just had to agree.

Carnival
An imprint of the Children's Division
of the Collins Publishing Group
8 Grafton Street, London W1X 3LA

Published by Carnival 1988

ISBN: 0 00 194520 3

Printed & bound in Great Britain by
PURNELL BOOK PRODUCTION LIMITED
A MEMBER OF BPCC plc